Whose Pet Is Best?

Mr. Lizard told Nancy to begin her trick.

"Okay, Chip," Nancy said. "Do your thing."

She kicked the soccer ball to her puppy. But Chip didn't do her trick. She just whimpered and sniffed at the ball. Then she scratched her nose and backed off.

"Come on, Chip," Nancy said. "Get the ball!"

Chip lay down and put her chin between her paws.

Nancy felt her heart beat fast. Something is wrong with my puppy, Nancy thought. Something horribly, terribly, awfully wrong!

The Nancy Drew Notebooks

Available from MINSTREL Books

THE
NANCY DREW
NOTEBOOKS®

#17

Whose Pet Is Best?

CAROLYN KEENE
ILLUSTRATED BY ANTHONY ACCARDO

A MINSTREL® BOOK

Published by POCKET BOOKS

New York   London   Toronto   Sydney   Singapore

A MINSTREL PAPERBACK *Original*

A Minstrel Book published by
POCKET BOOKS, a division of Simon & Schuster Inc.
1230 Avenue of the Americas, New York, NY 10020

Copyright © 1997 by Simon & Schuster Inc.
Produced by Mega-Books, Inc.

ISBN: 0-671-56861-2

First Minstrel Books printing March 1997

10 9 8 7 6 5 4 3 2

NANCY DREW, THE NANCY DREW NOTEBOOKS, A MINSTREL BOOK and colophon are registered trademarks of Simon & Schuster Inc.

Cover art by Joanie Schwarz

Printed in the U.S.A.

Whose Pet Is Best?

1

Chip, Chip, Hooray!

Hey, kids, do you have a poodle that can doodle?" the man on television asked. "Or a snake that can shake? Does anyone out there have an amazing pet?"

"We do! We do!" Eight-year-old Nancy Drew and Katie Zaleski bounced up and down on the couch in Nancy's den.

"If you do, then come meet me, Mr. Lizard, at the Carl Sandburg Elementary School tomorrow at ten A.M.," the man continued. "For the Amazing Pet Contest."

Bess Marvin and her cousin George Fayne, Nancy's two best friends, jumped up from the couch and cheered. Nancy's puppy, Chocolate Chip, was going to be in the contest. So was Katie's parrot, Lester.

The four girls were all in the same third-grade class.

"And remember, kids," Mr. Lizard said. "The winning pet and its owner will appear live on TV—right here on *Mr. Lizard's Funhouse.*"

Mr. Lizard's Funhouse was Nancy's favorite television show. She loved the games, songs, and silly jokes. But most of all, she loved the funny man with the wild red hair—Mr. Lizard.

Katie clasped her hands. "I'd do anything to be on Mr. Lizard's show. I'd wear my baby picture around my neck! I'd even eat brussels sprout sandwiches!"

"Brussels sprout sandwiches?" George shook her bouncy dark curls. "Gross!"

"That's our show for today, kids,"

2

Mr. Lizard said. "But before we say goodbye, it's time for a little lizard dancing!"

"I knew he'd do the lizard dance," Katie squealed. "I knew it!"

Nancy and her friends did the lizard dance, too. They waved their fingers behind their heads and flicked their tongues in and out.

When the show was over, Nancy turned off the TV. "I can't believe Mr. Lizard is going to be in our very own school yard tomorrow."

Katie fell back on the couch and hugged her knees. "I don't think Lester and I will sleep a wink tonight.

Bess turned to Katie. "What are you and your parrot going to do in the contest?"

"Sing a song," Katie said proudly.

"I've heard Lester talk, but I've never heard him sing," Bess said.

"I have," Nancy said. "One time I watched Lester when Katie's little cousin Melvin visited her."

"Melvin is allergic to feathers," Katie

explained, "so Lester has to leave whenever he's around."

George whistled. "Wow! A talking, singing parrot. That's cool."

"Of course, Chip's got a great trick, too," Bess added quickly. "How's it going, Nancy?"

"Let's find Chip, and I'll show you," Nancy said.

"Chip—here, girl," Nancy called as the four friends walked out of the den and into the living room.

Hannah Gruen, the Drews' housekeeper, was scrubbing muddy paw prints off the couch.

"Uh-oh," Nancy said. "Did Chip jump on the couch with her dirty paws again?"

Hannah nodded. "Maybe you can teach Chip another trick—to keep off the furniture."

"I'm sorry, Hannah," Nancy said. "Where's Chip now?"

"I put her in the yard," Hannah said. "She can't cause much trouble out there."

Nancy led her friends outside. Chip was tied to a tree with a long leash. She was lying in the shade. Someone else was in the yard, too—Brenda Carlton.

"What are you doing here, Brenda?" Nancy asked.

Brenda flipped her dark hair over her shoulder. "I'm writing a story about the Amazing Pet Contest for my newspaper.

The *Carlton News* was Brenda's own newspaper. Her father helped her type it on their home computer every week.

"You *have* seen the latest issue, haven't you?" Brenda asked the girls.

"Yeah," Katie whispered to Nancy. "At the bottom of Lester's birdcage."

"I heard that, Katie," Brenda said. She turned to Nancy. "By the way, Nancy, what trick did you teach your dog? What's her name—Oatmeal Raisin? Cherry Vanilla?"

"Her name is *Chocolate Chip*," Nancy said as she unhooked the leash from Chip's collar. "And we were just about to practice."

"Mind if I watch?" Brenda asked sweetly. It was a fake kind of sweet.

Nancy shrugged her shoulders and picked up a soccer ball from the ground. She stood in front of the goal she had set up, looked at Chip, and called out, "Stay." Then Nancy kicked the ball to her puppy.

Chip nuzzled the ball. She flipped it in the air with her nose and bounced it on her head. When the ball was high, Chip rolled on her back and kicked the ball with her hind feet. It flew into the net.

"Goal!" George cried.

"Totally awesome," Katie said.

Nancy turned to Brenda. "Will we be reading about Chip in the *Carlton News?*"

Brenda forced a yawn. "A stupid dog trick does not make a good story. But if Chip fails and makes a fool of her owner," Brenda said, "now, *that's* a good story."

Nancy glared at Brenda. "That will never happen."

Brenda flashed a mean smile. *"Anything* can happen."

"What type of tricks are the other pets doing?" Bess asked.

"I heard Orson Wong is bringing a flea circus to the contest," Katie said.

"No way." Nancy giggled.

"Uh-oh. Speaking of insects." George pointed over Nancy's shoulder. "Look who's coming."

Nancy turned and saw Jason Hutchings and David Berger enter her yard. They were famous for playing jokes on all the kids at school.

"What's so funny?" David asked.

"We were talking about Mr. Lizard's Amazing Pet Contest," Nancy said.

"David has a pet in the contest, too," Jason said.

"What kind of pet?" Nancy asked.

"A rat," David said.

"EEEEeeeeeewwwww!" the girls all screamed at once.

"His name is Skeevy." David made crawling movements with his fingers. "And he stands on his hind legs and begs for cheese."

7

Jason laughed and picked up Chip's soccer ball.

"Put that down," Nancy said. "That's part of Chip's trick."

"So what? Chip's not going to win anyway." Jason held the soccer ball over his head. "Skeevy is."

Chip barked and jumped at the ball. It was too high for her to reach.

"Hey, Jason, throw it here!" David yelled. He was jumping up and down next to Nancy's house.

"Okay, you asked for it." Jason threw the ball to David—hard.

Nancy held her breath as she watched the ball sail over David's head and crash through the living room window.

"You two are in big trouble!" Bess shouted to the boys.

"We're outta here," David said as he and Jason ran from the yard.

Then Chip bolted toward the house. When she got close, she yelped and leaped right through the broken window.

"Chip!" Nancy cried. "No!"

9

2

Chip's Big Break

Nancy and her friends rushed into the house.

"Wait for me!" Brenda called.

When the girls reached the living room, they saw broken glass scattered on the floor by the window.

"That broken window is bad enough," Hannah scolded Nancy. "But look what your puppy did to your father's favorite chair."

Nancy was afraid to look, but she did. The soccer ball was on the chair. So was Chocolate Chip—muddy paws and all.

"Not again." Nancy groaned. "Well, at least Chip's not hurt."

Chip buried her face in her paws.

"See, Nancy?" Brenda said. *Anything* can happen."

After the girls left, Nancy helped Hannah scrub the chair.

That evening Jason and David were sent over by their parents to apologize. Jason's father had insisted on paying for a new window. Nancy practiced Chip's trick in the yard. She was careful not to go near any of the windows.

The next morning Nancy woke up early. She dressed in her favorite jeans and a soccer shirt. It was Saturday—the day of the Amazing Pet Contest.

After Hannah's "good luck" breakfast, Mr. Drew drove Nancy and Chip to the school. They stopped to pick up Bess and George on the way.

"Why can't the school yard look like this every day?" Bess asked after Mr. Drew had dropped them off.

A large crowd had gathered by a big

wooden stage. Over the stage was a sign that read, Mr. Lizard's Amazing Pet Contest. Balloons were tied to the chain-link fence. They fluttered back and forth in the breeze.

Nancy didn't see Katie in the crowd of kids and pets. But she did see someone else.

"It's him!" Nancy cried. She pointed to the stage. "It's Mr. Lizard!"

Mr. Lizard was wearing a shiny green tuxedo jacket. A woman in a blue suit was standing next to him.

George sighed. "Pinch me. I must be dreaming."

"I want to get Mr. Lizard to sign my soccer ball," Nancy said to Bess and George. "Could you guys stay here and watch Chip for me? I don't want Mr. Lizard to see her before her trick."

Nancy handed Chip's leash to George and rushed to the stage. But she stopped when she noticed that Mr. Lizard and the woman were arguing. Nancy quickly ducked behind a nearby tree.

"I can't understand why you don't want a dog on the show," Nancy heard the woman say.

"Jane, you're my producer," Mr. Lizard said. "It's bad enough I have to do a dog food commercial with some pooch."

Nancy peeked out from behind the tree. Mr. Lizard didn't seem as nice in person as he did on TV. Even worse, it sounded as if he didn't like dogs.

"But there's a dog in the contest who plays soccer," Jane said.

"I don't care if it plays the accordion," Mr. Lizard snapped. "No more dogs."

"I'm sorry," Jane said. "But if a dog wins, a dog appears on the show."

"Yes!" Nancy whispered to herself. She knew that Mr. Lizard would change his mind once he saw Chip's trick.

Nancy decided to forget about the autograph and get back to her puppy. As she walked back she noticed that Bess and George were not paying at-

14

tention to Chip. They were watching a clown make balloon animals.

Then Nancy saw something worse. Brenda Carlton was kneeling next to Chip and feeding her a cookie!

"Brenda Carlton, drop that cookie," Nancy shouted, running toward them. "Sweets aren't good for dogs!"

Brenda stood up. A sneaky smile was on her face. "But her name *is* Chocolate Chip. And she really seems to like it."

"Sorry, Nancy," George said. "We just looked away for a minute."

"That clown was making a whole elephant out of one balloon," Bess added.

Just then Nancy heard Mr. Lizard's voice on the loudspeaker.

"Attention, kids," Mr. Lizard said. "The contest is about to begin. Will all contestants and their pets please line up in front of the stage?"

Nancy grabbed Chip's leash and made her way toward the stage. "See you guys after the show," she said to Bess and George.

Nancy saw Katie standing in line.

She was dressed as a pirate. She wore an eye patch and a bright red bandanna.

Lester sat perched on Katie's shoulder. He was wearing a tiny bandanna, too.

"Would you still do anything to win, Katie?" Nancy asked as she took her place behind her friend.

Katie lifted her eye patch. "Aaaaarrrrgh you kidding?" she said. "I'd even walk the plank!"

Lester bobbed his head. "Walk the plank. Walk the plank. *Squaaaaaawk!*"

Nancy heard the crowd cheer. She looked up and saw Mr. Lizard wiggling around the stage, dancing the lizard dance.

"Our first act, if you please," Mr. Lizard said into the microphone. "Orson Wong and his incredible fleas!"

A table with a tiny trapeze was set up on the stage.

Orson Wong ran to the table. He was dressed as a circus ringmaster. In one hand he held a wand. In the other, he held a bag marked Fleas.

"Ladies and gentlemen, prepare to be amazed!" Orson shouted. He shook the bag of fleas over the trapeze. Then he waved his wand in the air.

"Nancy, look," Katie whispered. "The trapeze is moving!"

Nancy watched the tiny trapeze swinging back and forth.

"There really aren't any fleas," Nancy whispered. "Orson is moving the trapeze with a magnet. Watch his hand under the table."

Katie tilted her head. "Wow, Nancy. You really are the school's best detective."

Nancy smiled. She liked solving mysteries.

When Orson's trick was over, Mr. Lizard called Katie and Lester up to the stage.

"Lester and I would like to sing a song we made up," Katie announced. "It's called, 'Me and My Pirate Parrot.'"

Nancy listened as Katie and Lester sang in perfect harmony. When they were finished, someone tapped her on the shoulder. Nancy turned her head and saw Orson Wong.

"Just how cool were my fleas?" Orson asked. He waved the bag in front of Nancy's face.

"Those aren't real fleas, Orson," Nancy said. "I saw your hand moving under the table."

"Oh, yeah?" Orson said. He yanked the bag open. "Tell that to your dog when she starts scratching like crazy." Orson held the bag over Chip.

"Don't you dare, Orson Wong," Nancy said. "I'm warning you."

But it was too late. Orson was already shaking the bag over Chocolate Chip's head!

3

Terrible Trick

Quit it, Orson!" Nancy shouted.

"Why? I thought you said my fleas weren't real." Orson laughed and disappeared into the crowd.

Nancy knelt down and brushed Chip's shiny brown coat with her hand.

"Of course those weren't fleas," Nancy whispered to her puppy. "Who ever heard of a real flea circus?"

When Nancy stood up, David Berger was standing right in front of her.

"Good luck, Nancy," David said. "You'll need it." He was holding Skeevy in a metal cage.

Jason Hutchings stood next to David. He had on a big purple backpack.

"Thanks," Nancy said. She tried not to look at the rat. "And may the best dog, I mean, pet win."

"You wish," David said.

Nancy wasn't going to let the boys spoil her fun. She turned back toward the stage just as Katie and Lester were coming down.

"That was Katie and Lester," Mr. Lizard shouted to the cheering crowd. "Now it's time for Nancy Drew and her mutt, Chocolate Chip."

Chip isn't a mutt, Nancy thought. She's a Labrador retriever.

Nancy clutched the soccer ball under her arm. Then she led Chip up the steps to the stage.

"Go for it, Nancy!" George called out from the crowd.

Nancy raised her finger over Chip's head. "Stay," she ordered gently. Then she took a few steps back and placed the ball on the stage floor.

Just as Nancy was about to kick the

ball to Chip, someone in the audience screamed.

"There's a rat!"

"Skeevy," David Berger called from the crowd. "Get back here."

Nancy didn't know what to do. Should she go on with her trick? Suddenly Nancy felt something furry brush against her ankle. She looked down to see Skeevy scrambling over her shoe.

"Eeeeeeeek!" Nancy stomped her foot. "Get off me!"

Chip barked and ran after Skeevy as the rat scurried across the stage.

"Chip, come back," Nancy shouted. She ran off the stage after Chip.

"Get the rat!" a little girl cried.

"He's too fast!" a boy yelled.

Nancy tried to catch Chip, but it was no use. Her puppy was lost in a crowd of kids and pets going wild!

"Stay calm, everyone," Jane shouted into the microphone. "And *please,* hold on to your pets!"

It was already much too late for that. Laura Anderson's cat was scrambling

up the jungle gym. Kenny Bruder's ferret was inching its way up the flagpole. A hamster was burrowing into the dirt in the playing field.

Nancy saw Brenda scribbling on a pad.

"Hi, Nancy. My story is going to be great!" Brenda said.

Nancy turned away. The last thing she wanted to think about was the *Carlton News*. She had to find Chip.

Nancy started to run but didn't get far. She crashed right into George.

"Where's Bess?" Nancy said.

George pointed to the jungle gym. Bess was sitting on the highest bar.

"Bess, I thought you were afraid of heights," Nancy called up to her.

"That was yesterday," Bess called back. "Today I'm afraid of *rats*."

"Can you see Chip from up there?" Nancy asked.

"I can see *everything* from up here," Bess answered. "Chip's on the stage."

Nancy ran back. Katie was standing with Chip on the stage. Lester was on

Katie's arm. "Good girl," Nancy said as she knelt down and petted her dog. Chip licked Nancy's nose.

"I found Chip running around by the swings," Katie said. "I walked her back here so you could finish your trick."

"Thanks, Katie." Nancy smiled. "You're the best."

Lester let out a loud screech. "You're the best! You're the best! *Arrrrk!*"

"Good luck, Nancy," Katie said with a giggle and walked off the stage.

Nancy was about to give Chip a big hug when she noticed a red cloth on the floor next to Chip's soccer ball. It was Katie's pirate bandanna.

Nancy picked it up and stuffed it into the pocket of her jeans. She would give it back to Katie after the contest.

Finally, Mr. Lizard returned to the stage. "The rat has been caught," he told the crowd. "Now, find your pets, and we'll go on with the show."

He told Nancy to begin again.

"Okay, Chip," Nancy said. "Do your thing."

She kicked the soccer ball to her puppy. But Chip didn't do her trick. She just whimpered and sniffed at the ball. Then she scratched her nose and backed off.

"Come on, Chip," Nancy said. "Get the ball!"

Chip lay down and put her chin between her paws.

Nancy felt her heart beat fast. Something is wrong with my puppy, Nancy thought. Something horribly, terribly, awfully wrong!

4

Sniffing for Clues

Nancy carried Chip down from the stage. Chip was still whimpering and scratching her nose.

Bess and George met Nancy at the bottom of the stage.

"Nice try, Nancy," George said, patting Nancy on the back.

"Um, yeah," Bess said. "You looked really great up there."

"Thanks," Nancy mumbled. She felt a huge lump in her throat as she tried not to cry.

The rest of the contest went by in an

awful blur. Nancy could barely stand to watch.

"Thanks, kids," Mr. Lizard said when the last act was over. "And thanks to your fine feathered and fur-faced friends."

Chip nuzzled her nose into the palm of Nancy's hand.

"Now it's time to announce the winner," Mr. Lizard said, "and the most amazing pet."

To everyone's delight, a chimpanzee ran onto the stage wearing a funny cap.

Even Nancy had to smile as the chimp handed Mr. Lizard an envelope, tipped his hat, and skipped off the stage.

"And the winner is," Mr. Lizard said, opening the envelope, "Katie Zaleski and her parrot, Lester."

The crowd cheered as Katie let out a scream and raced up the steps to join Mr. Lizard. "Oh, thank you, Mr. Lizard," she said. "This is the best day of my life."

Lester bobbed his head up and down. "Best day of my life. *Squawwwwwk!*"

Mr. Lizard announced the date Katie would be on the show. Then he lizard danced right off the stage. Soon Bess's mother drove up in her minivan to take Nancy, Bess, and George home. As the minivan pulled away, Nancy cradled Chip in her arms.

"We have to get home right away," Nancy said to Mrs. Marvin. "Chip is sick."

Nancy looked at her puppy. Chip didn't look good.

Chip was fine before the contest, Nancy thought. I wonder if someone made her sick. But who?

As soon as she got home, Nancy told her father what had happened at the pet contest. Carson Drew was a lawyer and often helped Nancy with her mysteries.

"Daddy, what if Orson *did* spill real fleas all over Chip?" Nancy asked.

Mr. Drew ruffled Nancy's reddish blond hair. "Remember, Pudding Pie. A good detective gathers *all* the evidence before closing a case."

"You're right." Nancy sighed. "Well, Brenda Carlton fed Chip a cookie before the contest. Maybe that made Chip sick."

Nancy's eyes lit up. "Or David might have opened Skeevy's cage on purpose so Chip would chase the rat. Or so Skeevy would bite Chip and keep her from doing her trick."

Mr. Drew laughed. "I think you'd better take Chip to see Dr. Rios to find out for sure."

Dr. Rios was Chip's veterinarian.

"Okay, Daddy." Nancy picked up her special blue detective's notebook. She used it to help her solve mysteries. "I'm taking this along just in case."

Nancy phoned Bess and George. She asked them to meet her at Dr. Rios's office with their bicycles.

Just as Nancy was about to go to the garage to get her bike, the doorbell rang. Nancy opened the door and saw

Katie Zaleski holding Lester in his cage.

"Hi, Nancy," Katie said. "You're not going to believe who just came by for a visit."

"Don't tell me," Nancy said. "Your cousin Melvin."

"Of all the days for him to visit," Katie said. "I should be celebrating with Lester, not dropping him off with you."

"You're dropping Lester off here?" Nancy asked. "Now?"

"Please, Nancy," Katie said. "It's just until dinnertime."

Nancy reached for the cage. "Okay. But I'm taking Chip to the vet. Is it all right if I leave Lester alone in the den?"

"Sure, Nancy. I knew I could count on you." Katie gave Nancy a playful punch in the arm and dashed off.

Nancy, Bess, and George watched quietly as Dr. Rios examined Chocolate Chip. When he was through, Dr. Rios turned to Nancy and smiled.

"You'll be happy to know that Chip was not bitten by a rat. Nor does she have fleas."

"But why was Chip scratching her face so much, Dr. Rios?" Nancy asked.

"I did find something sticky on Chip's nose," Dr. Rios said.

"Brenda's cookie," Nancy cried. "I knew it!"

Dr. Rios shook his head. "It's not a cookie, Nancy."

"Then what is it?" Nancy asked.

"It's something used to keep dogs away from things," Dr. Rios said. "It's called Paws Off."

"What's that?" Nancy asked.

"It's a kind of spray that only dogs can smell," Dr. Rios explained.

"Does it smell bad?" Nancy asked.

"It sure does," Dr. Rios said. "Paws Off is to dogs what sweaty gym socks are to people."

Nancy wrinkled her nose and laughed. "That *is* bad!"

Dr. Rios continued to explain. "People use Paws Off to keep dogs away from flower beds, baby carriages—"

"And soccer balls?" Nancy interrupted the doctor.

"Yes," Dr. Rios said. "I suppose so. In any case, your puppy is in good health. You have nothing to worry about."

"That's a relief," Nancy said. "Thanks, Dr. Rios. Bye."

Once the girls were outside the office, George turned to Nancy.

"Do you think someone at the contest sprayed Chip's soccer ball with Paws Off?"

Nancy nodded. "Definitely. I smell a rat," she said. "And it's not Skeevy."

5

Things Get Hairy

The girls leaned their bicycles against a bench in the park and sat down on the grass. Nancy held on to Chip's leash and opened her blue notebook.

"A mystery," Bess exclaimed. "Cool!"

Nancy wrote "The Amazing Pet Contest Mystery" on a fresh page.

"The best time for someone to have sprayed the soccer ball was when I left it to chase Chip," Nancy said.

She wrote "Suspects" on the next line.

"Well, Orson's not a suspect," Nancy said. "He was just playing a joke on

34

me with his fake fleas. I almost believed him, too."

"Then who is?" Bess asked.

"My first suspect is Brenda Carlton," Nancy said, writing Brenda's name in her book. "She really wanted Chip to mess up so she could write about it."

"How Brenda-ish!" Bess groaned.

"Then there are David and Jason," Nancy added. "Maybe they let Skeevy loose on purpose so they could spray the soccer ball. They're always playing tricks."

Nancy wrote the boys' names under Brenda's.

"Jason was also wearing his backpack," Nancy added. "He could have hidden *ten* cans of Paws Off in there."

"Did I hear my name?" a voice said. Nancy looked up and saw Jason Hutchings and David Berger. She quickly closed her notebook.

David was holding Skeevy's cage. Jason had his big purple backpack slung over one shoulder.

"How's Scratchy doing?" Jason asked. He laughed and gave David a high five.

"If you mean Chocolate Chip," George snapped, "she's fine."

Nancy grabbed Chip's leash. She, Bess, and George marched over to Jason and David. "You let Skeevy out of his cage on purpose, didn't you?" Nancy said.

"Maybe," Jason said. "Maybe not."

"Don't bother asking Skeevy," David said, holding the cage closer to the girls. "He would never *rat* on us."

Nancy, Bess, and George jumped back. Chip tugged at her leash and growled at David.

"Down, girl," Nancy ordered.

David passed the cage to Jason and backed away. Chip tried to reach the cage by jumping up on Jason's leg.

"Get her off me!" Jason shouted.

Bess giggled. "Jason's afraid of puppies! Jason's afraid of puppies!"

Chip jumped on Jason again. Jason's purple backpack slipped off his shoul-

der and fell to the ground. Everything inside spilled out.

"See what she made me do?" Jason said. "Dumb dog."

"Serves you right," George said. "You were teasing her!"

"Was not!" Jason yelled.

"Was, too!" George yelled back.

Nancy didn't argue. She was too busy staring at the spilled backpack.

"Bess, George," Nancy said, pulling Chip to her side. "Why don't we help Jason clean up this mess?"

"No way, Jose!" Bess shouted.

"What for?" George asked.

Nancy smiled slyly. "Because you never know what you'll find," she whispered.

The girls picked up Jason's stuff piece by piece. They found two packs of bubble gum, a rubber spider, and a water bottle. Nancy picked up a wet paper bag. It smelled yucky.

"Gross! What is this?" Nancy asked, holding her nose.

"It's Skeevy's lunch," David said. "He likes blue cheese with onions."

"That's disgusting," George said.

Nancy shoved the paper bag into the backpack and sighed. There was no can of Paws Off anywhere.

"Forget it," Nancy whispered. "This backpack is clueless."

The girls brushed off their hands. They stood up and returned to their bikes.

"You can clean up our rooms next," David teased.

"No way," George shouted back. "I'd rather clean a hippopotamus's toenails!"

After pedaling a few blocks, the girls stopped their bikes in front of a small glass building. It was the local television station, WRIV-TV.

Nancy looked up at the building. "This is where Mr. Lizard does his show," she said.

"And those dog food commercials." Bess giggled. "They're funny."

All of a sudden, Nancy remembered that Mr. Lizard had said he didn't want another dog act on his show. Could he have used the Paws Off?

"I think I might have another suspect," Nancy said to her friends.

"What do you mean?" Bess asked.

They hitched their bikes to a rack in front of the building while Nancy explained.

"It won't be easy," Nancy said. "But let's try to speak to Mr. Lizard."

The girls walked through the main door of the television studio. Nancy led the way, holding Chip's leash tightly.

A guard in a blue uniform sat behind a desk. She looked at the girls and smiled. "Hello. You must be the kid reporter Mr. Lizard is expecting."

"Uh, I am?" Nancy asked.

George nudged Nancy.

"Yes, I am!" Nancy said quickly.

The guard handed Nancy, Bess, and George three visitor's passes.

"Third floor, to your left," she said, pointing to an elevator.

"Are we lucky or what?" George whispered to Nancy.

The girls rode the elevator up to the third floor. The doors opened, and they stepped out.

Nancy spotted a door with a shiny gold star. Mr. Lizard's name was on it. "This is Mr. Lizard's dressing room." She made sure Chip stayed close to her.

Bess gazed at the star. "This is where he combs his bushy red hair."

"And puts on those big rubber ears," George said.

"And this is where he might hide a can of Paws Off," Nancy said.

"I hope Mr. Lizard didn't do it," George said.

The door was open a crack. Nancy peeked in and saw the room was empty.

Nancy turned to Bess and George. "There's only one way to find out."

"You mean go in?" Bess asked. "Going into Mr. Lizard's dressing room would be like going into—the White House!"

"We have to," Nancy said.

The three girls slipped through the door and looked around. There was a big mirror on the wall and lots of colorful costumes and hats on a rack.

George patted her chest. "My heart feels like it's doing the lizard dance."

Bess slipped her feet into a pair of giant red-and-white shoes. "How can anyone do the lizard dance in these things?" she said.

Nancy walked over to a long, white table. On it was a row of bushy red wigs set on fake heads. Next to the wigs was a large spray can. Could it be Paws Off? Nancy wondered.

She picked up the can to look at the label. It was a product called Hair Today.

Suddenly, George grabbed Nancy's arm. "I hear someone coming. Quick, let's hide!"

Nancy grabbed Chocolate Chip and picked her up. Then she, George, and Bess ducked behind a costume rack.

Chip grunted softly.

"Shhhhh," Nancy whispered into the dog's ear.

The girls peeked out from behind a shiny purple-and-gold cape.

Nancy watched as a man entered the room. He was dressed like Mr. Lizard but didn't look like him. This man was totally bald.

The man walked over to the mirror. He looked at himself and rubbed his head. Then he reached for the can of Hair Today and sprayed his entire head.

"Yuck! What is he doing?" Bess whispered to Nancy.

Nancy saw the man grab a bushy red wig and place it on his head.

"It *is* Mr. Lizard!" she hissed.

Nancy felt her heart sink. Not only was Mr. Lizard not as nice as he was on TV, but his wild red hair wasn't even real.

"Nancy." George sniffled. "That stinky spray is tickling my nose."

Nancy looked at George in horror.

"Don't sneeze, George," Nancy pleaded. "Whatever you do, don't—"

"*AHHHHHCCCHOOOOOOO!*"

Nancy, Bess, and George froze.

"Who's back there?" Mr. Lizard roared.

6

Polly Wanna Crack a Case?

Y ou might as well come out," Mr. Lizard called. "I know you're behind that costume rack!"

"How does he know where we are?" Bess murmured.

Nancy pointed to the floor. "You forgot to take off the giant shoes."

Bess looked down. The clown shoes were sticking out from under the costumes.

"Whoops." Bess slipped her feet out of the big shoes. "Sorry."

The girls slowly stepped out from behind the costumes.

Mr. Lizard looked at them and crossed his arms. Then Jane, the producer, stepped into the dressing room.

"What is going on here?" Jane asked. She looked at Nancy and Chip. "What are you two doing here?"

"Uh, I'm here to ask Mr. Lizard a few questions," Nancy said.

Mr. Lizard nodded. "Oh, yeah. You must be the kid reporter who's supposed to interview me, right?"

Nancy's mouth felt as if it were full of cotton. She had to think fast.

"Yes," Nancy said. She opened her notebook and took a pencil out of her jeans pocket. "I promise not to take up much of your time."

"No problem," Mr. Lizard said. "Ask me anything you want."

"First question," Nancy said. "What do you think of the product Paws Off?"

"Paws Off?" Mr. Lizard said. "Never heard of it."

Nancy stared at Mr. Lizard. I wonder if he's telling the truth?

Nancy twirled the pencil between her

fingers. She pointed it at Mr. Lizard's head. "Next question. That hair of yours—is it real?"

A hush fell over the dressing room. Jane followed Mr. Lizard as he paced back and forth, biting his nails.

Mr. Lizard sighed and turned to Nancy. He yanked the wig off his head. "Does this answer your question?"

Nancy smiled. Mr. Lizard may be a gruff man, she thought, but at least he's honest.

"Just one more question, Mr. Lizard," Nancy said. "Do you like having dogs on your show?"

Jane chuckled. "Good question!"

"Okay, I have to admit it," Mr. Lizard said. "I'm not too crazy about mutts."

Mr. Lizard reached down and patted Chip gently. "Except for this little one. She has to be the cutest puppy I've ever seen."

Nancy's eyes twinkled with excitement. That was all she needed to hear.

"Thank you, Mr. Lizard." Nancy closed

her notebook and put her pencil in her pocket. "No more questions."

"That was the shortest interview I've ever given," Mr. Lizard said.

"Bye," Nancy said.

The girls and Chip left the dressing room and rode the elevator back down to the first floor.

Brenda Carlton was standing by the guard's desk. The guard was holding a walkie-talkie.

"I think I have a way to find out if Brenda sprayed the Paws Off," Nancy said to Bess and George as they walked toward Brenda.

"How?" George asked.

"We have to play a trick," Nancy said. "Just follow along with what I do."

"Okay." Bess smiled. "This is going to be fun."

"I'm sorry, miss," the guard said to Brenda. "But Mr. Lizard just gave an interview to a young reporter."

"That's impossible!" Brenda cried.

Then Brenda looked at Nancy.

"What are you and Chocolate Marshmallow doing here?" Brenda asked.

"Chocolate *Chip!*" Bess snapped.

"We were just coming from *Mr. Lizard's Funhouse*," Nancy said. "His producer has a video of the whole contest."

Brenda's eyes were wide. "What's in the video?"

"Everything." Nancy leaned in close to Brenda. "Even what *you* did."

Brenda twirled her brown hair around her finger. "So what? Skeevy didn't hurt anyone."

Nancy's eyebrows shot up. "Skeevy?"

"Mr. Lizard should thank me for letting the rat out of the cage," Brenda continued. "It was the most exciting thing in that whole contest."

"You let Skeevy out of the cage?" George asked.

Brenda nodded. "And I'd do it again. It made a great story."

"And you sprayed Paws Off on my soccer ball for your story, too," Nancy said. "So Chip wouldn't do her trick."

Brenda stared at Nancy. "Stop making excuses for your dumb dog," Brenda sneered. "I had nothing to do with it."

"Chocolate Chip is not dumb." Bess bent down to give Nancy's puppy a hug.

Nancy didn't want to, but she believed Brenda. If she had used the Paws Off, she probably would have bragged about that, too.

"Let's go," Nancy told Bess and George. "Oh, by the way," Nancy said to Brenda as they walked past. "Mr. Lizard gives the coolest interviews."

Before Brenda could say another word, Nancy and her friends were out the door.

Later Nancy, Bess, and George sat on the floor in the Drews' den. Hannah had gone to spend the night at her sister's house. Mr. Drew was in the kitchen, cooking a spaghetti dinner.

"Well, that rules out Mr. Lizard," Nancy said, scratching his name out of her book. "He's very honest, and he really likes Chip."

"I'm glad Mr. Lizard didn't do it," Bess said. "I would hate to have to stop doing the lizard dance."

"The boys are off the hook, too," Nancy said, crossing off their names. "There was no spray can in Jason's backpack. And they didn't let Skeevy out of his cage—Brenda did."

"Are you sure that Brenda didn't spray the soccer ball?" George asked.

Nancy nodded and crossed off Brenda's name. "I'm sure," she said.

"So who did it, Nancy?" Bess asked.

"I don't know," Nancy said. She stared down at her list. "We have no more suspects. And I can't think of anyone else who might have wanted Chip and me to lose the contest."

"Let's take a break from detective work, Nan," George said.

"Yeah," Bess said. "Let's play with Lester!"

"Arrrrrrk," Lester squawked, rolling his colorful neck as Nancy, Bess, and

George walked over to the parrot's cage.

"Let's teach Lester a new song so we can surprise Katie when she comes to pick him up," Nancy said. "Here's one I learned from Hannah called, 'Friendship.' "

Nancy sang the first line. " 'If you're ever in a jam, here I am!' "

Lester looked at Nancy and blinked.

"You're supposed to be a talking, singing parrot," Bess said. "Say something."

Lester stared at the girls. Then he screeched, "Paws Off. Paws Off. Does the trick. *Arrrrrrk!*"

7

The Unusual Suspect

Did you say Paws Off?" George asked Lester. She touched the bars of the cage.

Lester tilted his head from side to side. "Ohhhhh-boy," he screeched.

"I didn't mention Paws Off in front of Lester," Nancy said. She whirled around to Bess and George. "Did either of you?"

Bess and George shook their heads.

"Whoever said 'Paws Off' in front of Lester probably used it." Nancy sat back down on the floor and grabbed her blue notebook.

"But who?" Bess asked.

Nancy felt something being tugged out of her back pocket. She turned to see Chip with the red bandanna in her mouth.

"Katie's bandanna," Nancy said. She took the cloth from Chip's mouth. "I found it near the soccer ball during the contest."

"You did?" Bess asked. "When?"

"After the Skeevy chase," Nancy said, "and right before Chip's trick."

Nancy thought for a minute.

"What is it, Nancy?" George asked.

"Katie was by the soccer ball right before Chip's trick," Nancy said. "Alone."

Nancy wrote Katie's name in her notebook. Next to her name she wrote "Lester" and "red bandanna."

"Katie also said she'd do anything to win," Nancy said.

"She said she'd eat brussels sprout sandwiches," George said, "not spray Chip's soccer ball with Paws Off."

"George is right," Bess said. "Katie would never do a mean thing like that."

"Don't you see?" Nancy said. "Katie must have said, 'Paws Off does the trick.' And Lester repeated it. Lester is *always* repeating what Katie says!"

The doorbell rang and Chip barked.

"That's probably Katie now," Nancy said. She stuffed the bandanna back into her pocket and picked up Lester's cage.

Bess and George followed Nancy as she answered the front door.

"Thanks for looking after Lester, Nancy," Katie said.

"You're welcome," Nancy said, still standing in the doorway.

"Did Chip's checkup go okay?" Katie asked with a smile.

"Not really," Nancy said. "The vet found something called Paws Off on Chip's nose. Someone sprayed it on her soccer ball so she wouldn't do her trick."

Katie opened her eyes wide. "How

awful! Who would do a thing like that?"

"According to Lester," Nancy said, "you."

"Me?" Katie shrieked.

"Lester called out 'Paws Off,'" Nancy said. "Where did he hear that if not from you?"

"Nancy," Katie gasped. "I would never do a thing like that."

Nancy handed Katie her bandanna. "This was in Chip's mouth. I hope you don't mind dog spit."

"My pirate bandanna," Katie said. "I knew I dropped it when I brought Chip back to the stage."

"Or while you were spraying Chip's soccer ball with Paws Off," Nancy said.

"Nancy," Katie cried. "I'd rather hug a porcupine than do something awful to you!"

Nancy handed Lester's cage to Katie. "Here's your parrot, Katie, or should I say—stool pigeon?"

Bess and George looked at each

other. Then they watched as Nancy shut the door.

A second later Nancy heard Lester sing from the other side: " 'If you're ever in a jam, here I am!' *Squaaaaaawwwwk!*"

Nancy woke up early Sunday morning. She got dressed and went downstairs.

Mr. Drew was in the kitchen, reading the Sunday paper. Nancy had told him all about Katie the night before. "Blaming a friend is very serious, Nancy," her father said. "Are you sure about this?"

Nancy poured herself a bowl of cereal. "It's as clear as the itchy nose on Chip's face, Daddy."

She swallowed a mouthful of Crispy Crunchies. "I'm going to keep very busy today. The busier I am, the less I'll think about Katie Zaleski."

After eating, Nancy cleaned her room. She had decided to surprise Hannah by recycling the trash when she heard Bess and George knocking on the kitchen door. Nancy let them in.

"I just spoke to Katie on the phone," Bess said. "She's really upset."

"We think the whole thing stinks, Nancy," George added.

"Whose friends are you anyway?" Nancy cried.

"We're *your* friends," Bess said. "But we think you made a mistake."

"A mistake?" Nancy repeated. "But I'm the school's best detective. Remember?"

Nancy didn't want to argue anymore. She slipped on a pair of rubber gloves and knelt down by the recycle bin. Chip padded into the kitchen and over to Nancy.

"What are you doing?" George asked.

"Sorting the recyclable stuff," Nancy said. "Want to help?"

Bess made a face. "You mean go through garbage? That's even grosser than going through Jason Hutchings's backpack."

"Come on, Bess," Nancy said. "Let's see what's in here."

Nancy reached into the bin. She pulled out all the items one by one. "An empty bottle of cranberry juice, an old tuna fish can—"

"Eeeeew," Bess said, making a face.

Chip barked and licked her chops.

"This isn't recyclable," Nancy said, pulling out the next item. "It's an empty can of—"

Chip grunted and jumped back.

Nancy read the label and froze.

"Nancy, what is it?" George asked.

"Paws Off," Nancy gasped. "It's an empty can of Paws Off!"

8

Hannah Comes Clean

"How could Katie have thrown the can away here?" Nancy wondered out loud.

Suddenly Nancy heard Hannah's voice. "Nancy, I'm home," Hannah called.

Nancy stared at the can. "Could Hannah have used it?"

"No way," George said. "Hannah wanted Chip to win the contest."

"But she also wanted Chip to stay away from the furniture," Nancy said. "Remember?"

"What are you going to do, Nancy?" Bess asked.

"There's only one thing to do." Nancy tossed the can back into the bin. Then she led Bess and George to the front door to greet Hannah.

"Hi, girls!" Hannah said. She placed a small suitcase on the floor.

"Hannah, may I ask you something?" Nancy asked.

"Sure, Nancy," Hannah said with a grin. "Ask me anything."

Nancy took a deep breath. "Did you ever use a spray called Paws Off?"

Hannah nodded. "Oh, yes. I used it on the living room furniture yesterday morning while you were still asleep."

"You did?" Nancy asked.

"Yes, and I'm sure glad I did," Hannah said. "It's been a whole day, and there's not one muddy paw print on the furniture. That Paws Off really did the trick!"

For a moment Nancy felt her knees grow weak. Katie was innocent all along.

"Was Chip's soccer ball near the fur-

63

niture when you sprayed it?" Nancy asked Hannah.

Hannah nodded. "I saw it after I sprayed the chair. I put the ball outside in the yard," Hannah explained. "That's where you found it yesterday morning."

Bess clapped her hands.

It *was* Hannah who sprayed the soccer ball, Nancy thought. But then where did Lester learn how to say "Paws Off"?

"Just a few more questions, Hannah," Nancy said. "Did you talk about Paws Off with anyone yesterday?"

"I phoned my sister about it," Hannah said. "She has a problem with her golden retriever jumping on the beds."

Nancy took a deep breath. "Were you in the den when you spoke to your sister?"

"Hmmmm." Hannah rubbed her chin. "I believe I was."

Nancy's mouth dropped open.

"Nancy," Bess whispered. "You kept Lester's cage in the den yesterday."

"Can someone please tell me what's going on?" Hannah asked. "Am I some sort of suspect?"

Nancy explained everything to Hannah.

"I'm sorry, Nancy," Hannah said. "I should have told you I was going to use Paws Off. After all, Chip is your dog."

"That's okay, Hannah." Nancy smiled. "It was an accident."

Hannah gave Nancy a hug. "Well, if Paws Off caused all that trouble, we'll never use it again."

"But how will we keep Chip off the furniture?" Nancy asked.

"We can try this." Hannah looked at Chip. "Down, girl," she said sternly.

Chip's ears shot up. She whined and lowered her head.

"See? It might work," Hannah said.

The girls laughed along with Hannah. After Hannah headed for her room, Bess turned to Nancy.

"We'll go with you to Katie's house when you decide to apologize," Bess said.

"Of course I'm going to apologize," Nancy said. "I'm not afraid to say I was wrong."

George and Bess looked at each other and giggled.

"What's so funny?" Nancy asked.

Before George and Bess could explain, Nancy spotted Katie outside the window.

"Here comes Katie now," Nancy said. "I just hope she forgives me."

"I'll cross all my fingers," Bess said, scrunching up her hands.

"And I'll cross my eyes," George said, doing just that.

"Hi, Katie," Nancy said with a big smile. "I'm so happy you came by."

Katie stared at Nancy. "You are? Really?"

"Really," Nancy said. "I'm sorry I blamed everything on you. It was Hannah who sprayed the soccer ball with Paws Off."

"Hannah?" Katie gasped. "No way!"

"She didn't mean it," Nancy said. "It was an accident."

"Accidents will happen," Katie said.

"I know I acted like a creep, Katie," Nancy said, "but do you think we can be friends again?"

Katie smiled and reached into her pocket. She pulled out three small square cards and handed them to Nancy.

Nancy stared at the cards. "Three tickets for *Mr. Lizard's Funhouse.* Cool!"

"They're for you, Bess, and George," Katie said. "Lester and I could use a few fans the day we're on the show."

"We're all going to *Mr. Lizard's Funhouse?*" George asked.

Katie nodded and smiled.

"Let's lizard dance!" the four friends screamed together. They waved their fingers behind their heads and hopped up and down. Then they ran into the living room.

Chip barked and jumped up and down, too.

Hannah came back to see what they were doing. "I could hear you girls all the way from my room," she said with a grin.

Nancy grabbed Hannah's hand. "We're doing the lizard dance, Hannah. Come on, join us!"

Nancy showed Hannah the steps. Hannah repeated Nancy's motions. She waved her fingers behind her head and flicked her tongue in and out.

"I think I've got it," Hannah said, wiggling her hips. "Mr. Lizard—step aside!"

Nancy and her friends formed a circle around Hannah as she danced. "Go, Han-nah! Go, Han-nah! Go, Han-nah! Yay!"

That evening Nancy sat on her bed with her blue notebook. Chip lay on the floor, nibbling lightly on Nancy's fluffy pink slippers.

Nancy opened her book and turned to the page that said "The Amazing Pet Contest Mystery." On the bottom she wrote:

Daddy was right when he said I should gather *all* the evidence before closing a case!

I'm glad Katie and I are friends again. And I still like Mr. Lizard, even if his red hair isn't real. I guess even the biggest TV stars can have secrets.

And even the best detectives can make mistakes!

Case closed.

**Do your younger brothers and sisters
want to read books like yours?**

**Let them know there
are books just for *them!***

They can join Nancy Drew and her best
friends as they collect clues and solve
mysteries in

T H E

N A N C Y   D R E W

N O T E B O O K S ®

Starting with

#1 The Slumber Party Secret

#2 The Lost Locket

#3 The Secret Santa

#4 Bad Day for Ballet

AND

**Meet up with suspense and mystery
in The Hardy Boys® are: The Clues Brothers™**

Starting with

#1 The Gross Ghost Mystery

#2 The Karate Clue

#3 First Day, Worst Day

#4 Jump Shot Detectives

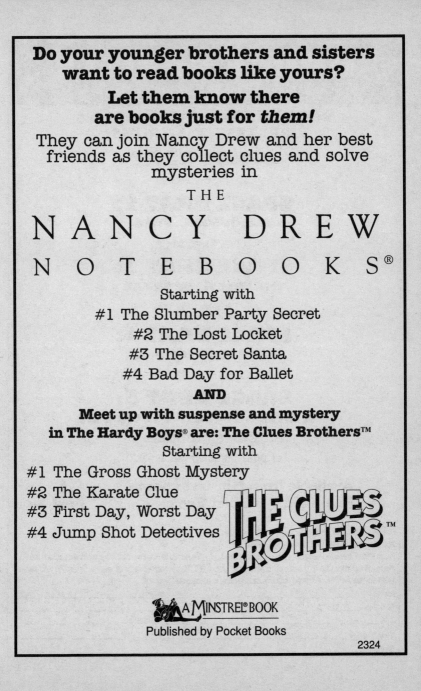

A MINSTREL® BOOK

Published by Pocket Books

2324